The Meaning of Life for Kids

An Adventure for All Ages

R. J. Albanese
E. T. Sherman

Illustrated by Michael Christon

The Meaning of Life for Kids
An Adventure for All Ages
ISBN 978-0-9916124-9-9
Copyright © 2021 R. J. Albanese and E. T. Sherman
www.rjalbanese.com

Art Direction and Cover Design: Diane Whisner
Illustrations: Michael Christon

Dear Reader,

This is a true story embedded in a fiction. Some license was taken with nonessentials, but the essentials remain true. To verify what is true, you can read The Meaning of Life, by R. J. Albanese, or just be like a Berean, those who studied to see if these things be true.

It is our hope that minds will be challenged and hearts expanded by our little story. We are certain, our lives have never been the same!

The Authors

Contents

1
The Map

"Get up and get going, kids! Grandma and Grandpa are excited to see you!" yelled Mom up the stairs. Rachel and Josh were twins, but they were very different. Josh immediately jumped out of bed, while Rachel rubbed her eyes and stared at the ceiling. She smiled, stretched, and slowly turned to sit on her bed. It was a beautiful day, spring was here, and like her brother, she couldn't wait to see her grandparents.

Grandma and Grandpa lived in the Blue Ridge Mountains of Virginia, and the twins loved to visit them. Grandpa told awesome stories (as Grandma rolled her eyes and grinned), and there were so many places to explore. At eleven years old, with the sun shining and the snow melted, they were ready to take on the world. Mom and Dad would be gone the entire week of spring break, celebrating their fifteenth anniversary. A whole week with Grandma and Grandpa!

They quickly dressed, ate their breakfast, and then ran upstairs. They brushed their teeth and put their toothbrushes and a few last items in their suitcases, which Mom had helped them pack. Soon, they were on their way, and the two-hour drive seemed to last forever. No electronics allowed in the car or at Grandma and Grandpa's. Vacation was for spending time with family, and in the car that meant talking, reading, car games, enjoying the scenery – and a lot of asking, "How much longer?"

Dad said, "Now, I know you will be on your best behavior, right?"

"Yes, Dad," the twins chimed.

"And obey your grandparents while we are

away?" said Mom.

"Yes, Mom," they vowed, squirming in their seats.

"How much longer? I don't remember going through these hills this long," said Josh.

"We're almost there. Be patient," said Dad.

Fifteen minutes later, they turned onto the winding, stone driveway and Dad honked the horn to let his parents know they had arrived. As the car stopped in front of the large log cabin, Grandma and Grandpa walked down the steps of the front porch toward the car, beaming with arms outstretched. The twins jumped out of the car and ran to hug them. Grandpa swung Rachel around and Grandma rocked Josh back and forth in a fierce hug.

"Hello! Hello! My, how you've grown!" cried Grandma.

"Won't be long and I won't be able to lift you!" said Grandpa.

Dad and Mom unloaded the twins' suitcases and backpacks, and everyone was hugging everyone else. "Can you stay a minute and have a snack before you go?" asked Grandma.

"Would love to, but we have to be at the airport by four," said Dad.

"Thank you so much for doing this," said Mom.

"Oh, for Pete's sake! You know we love having them. We've been on the edge of our seats ever since you called."

Dad and Mom kissed and hugged the twins, admonished them one more time to be good, and everyone waved as they drove off.

"What are we going to do today?" asked Josh. The twins noticed how Grandma and Grandpa looked at each other. A thrill of excitement ran through them. They knew that look! Something was up.

"Well, let's get you settled in the bunk room first," said Grandpa, grabbing the two suitcases and starting up the steps. Josh and Rachel knew their grandparents were old – after all, they were sixty – but they seemed really strong for their age. They also were really, really smart – and loads of fun.

Josh threw his backpack and jacket on the top bunk, and Rachel put her backpack on the bottom bunk, then went to the closet to hang up her jacket. Grandma peeked around the door and asked, "How about lunch?"

As they sat at the round, oak table in the kitchen, Grandma and Grandpa asked them about school, their activities, and their friends. They took turns answering, often interrupting each other. Their interests were so different, the only time they competed with one another was in getting someone's attention.

After the dishes were done, Grandpa disappeared for a while and then joined them in the living room. He carried a large, flat, cardboard box that used to be white. As he sank down in his worn recliner, Rachel asked, "What's in the box, Grandpa?"

"It's your assignment."

"Our assignment?" cried Josh.

"Like in school?" Rachel looked horrified. "I thought we were going to have fun!"

"Oh, don't worry, Sweetheart! You're going

to have more than fun. We are sending you on a great adventure!" Grandma said, smiling warmly at Grandpa.

The twins were still skeptical as Grandpa shook the box, his eyes twinkling. "This is the map to the treasure."

"Treasure! Wow! You mean, like pirate booty with gold coins and silver and jewels?" asked Josh.

"Better than that," answered Grandpa.

"Better than gold and jewels?" Rachel wondered how that could be.

Grandma rocked dreamily in her rocking chair. "Oh, these mountains are full of all kinds of treasures. When your grandpa and I were kids growing up here, I think we explored every forest, cave, and stream." She stopped rocking and leaned forward, her voice lowered. "Then one day, we came across this special treasure, and our lives were never the same."

"Yep. That's right," said Grandpa. "After we got back, we made this map, and we took turns keeping it safe until we married. Then we kept it for our kids and grandkids. One day, you may give it to your kids and grandkids."

"Dad and Mom never told us. Do they know? Have they seen the treasure too?" asked Rachel.

"Oh yes. But they wanted it to be a surprise," answered Grandma.

"Now, wait a minute," said Josh. "Aren't you coming with us?"

"No, this is your adventure, and we know you'll be safe, just like your parents were, and just like we were at your age." Grandpa had the "that's a fact" look on his face. He carefully removed the lid of the box and took out the map. It was a large piece of yellow construction paper with black ink lines, pictures, and writing. In the corner was a compass to indicate north, south, east, and west. The map had been laminated for protection, but it still looked old and worn.

The twins stood on either side of the recliner, leaning in to look at the strange markings. They recognized their grandparents' handwriting at different places. "Whoa…this is soooo amazing."

They spent the rest of the afternoon going over the map, trying to get as much information from their grandparents as they could. They knew their destination was a cave, but Grandma and Grandpa would not tell them what was inside or what the treasure was.

There were no stories from Grandpa that night, only bear hugs, kisses, and being tucked in so tightly they could hardly move. Grandma prayed for them, Grandpa turned out the lights, and they were soon dreaming about pirates, treasure maps, and chests of gold.

3 tall pines
arrowhead
on tree
Go 10
Straig
Swit
Rte 7981
Log crossing
X Start
Stream

eps
ead
the cave
N
W E
S
huge quartz boulder
backs
Due
East
Indian trail
at holly bush

2
The Cave

The twins awoke to the smell of pancakes, eggs, and bacon. They hurried to dress and get out to the kitchen to enjoy their favorites, and everyone was unusually quiet. Josh and Rachel knew their grandparents were not going to tell them anything more, and all they could think about was the map and the journey ahead of them. As they wiped their mouths and thanked Grandma for a delicious breakfast, she said, "I've packed your lunches, because you'll be hungry after hiking up that mountain."

"You've got a beautiful day for an adventure," Grandpa smiled. "Go empty your backpacks, so you just have to carry your lunch and water. Oh, and I have a flashlight for each of you." He rose and walked over to a kitchen drawer, where he pulled out two flashlights, one red and one green. Rachel took the red and Josh the green, their favorite colors, because they had been born on Christmas Day.

Grandma took a deep breath, was about to say something, stopped, and murmured to herself, "Yes, you will need flashlights part of the time."

Rachel heard what she said and saw an opening to find out something more.

"What do you mean, Grandma?"

"Just what she said," answered Grandpa, shaking his head and frowning at Grandma, as if to say, "Don't give anything away."

Suddenly Josh felt uncertain. "You know, Grandpa, usually you and Grandma go with us."

"Well Josh, you don't have to go if you don't want to," Grandma said as she removed the plates from the table.

"No, we want to go," he replied quickly, hiding his fear. He looked at Rachel, who also looked a little rattled. "Don't we?"

Rachel shrugged her shoulders and then said yes in her firmest voice. Now that they were about to leave, she realized what they had to do to get to the treasure. She was glad she didn't have to go alone.

The twins put on their jackets and backpacks. As Grandpa opened the front door, he gave the map to Josh and Grandma handed Rachel a compass. Their dad had taught the twins how to use a compass when they were old enough to read, just like Grandpa had taught him. "Now remember to count 100 steps and walk straight ahead after you're in the cave."

"And if you see anyone we know, please tell them hello," Grandma had tears in her eyes. Josh thought she was probably thinking of a neighbor she hadn't seen in a while, someone hiking in the mountains. After all, she was getting older and more sentimental.

"Okay, Grandma," Rachel hugged her and Grandpa, as did Josh, and they were on their way down the driveway. The map told them to cross the old, country road at the end of the driveway and turn north, following the stream that ran beside it. Josh held the map and Rachel held the compass like lifelines. Their hearts were soon at ease, however, because it was a good map. Every change in direction was clearly marked by some natural landmark and a compass direction. They walked north along the stream on a gradual, uphill climb. The sun was bright, and it wasn't long before they stopped to remove their jackets, put them in their backpacks, and take a drink.

About ten minutes later, they came to a huge tree that had fallen across the stream. The map directed them to cross the stream on the log, so they climbed up. They didn't really need to put their arms out to keep their balance, because the fallen tree trunk was so wide, but they did it out of habit and easily crossed over. On the other side of the stream, they were to continue going straight east until they reached an old Indian trail, where they would turn north again. Rachel checked the compass and the position of the sun, just like she and Josh had been taught, to make sure they were headed east. "We're a little off. Let's go more to our right. Okay, now we're going due east."

They had never been in this part of the forest, as most of their exploring had been on the other side of the road and nearer the cabin. The woods became even denser, with rays of sunlight piercing through, making everything seem magical. From time to time, they would see deer or wild turkeys. Once they were startled by something crashing through some bushes, but it turned out to be a family of squirrels. "God, please keep the bears away from us," said Rachel.

"Yes!" agreed Josh. He had a terrible thought. It was spring and the bears would be waking up from hibernation and be hungry. Better not tell Rachel.

The map showed that the winding path was just up ahead, and sure enough, they stumbled out of a lot of brush and found themselves on it. The old Indian trail was cleared brown earth, about four feet wide in most spots. They knew they were in the right spot because the map showed a holly bush in the middle of the trail, and it was surrounded by a circle of cleared earth, about five feet all around.

While studying the map with their grandparents, Grandpa had chuckled and pointed to the holly bush. "The Indians must have invented the roundabout!" Grandma and Grandpa had always had great respect for the people who first came to this land and kept it so well. Some of their best friends were of the Cherokee Nation, who had told them that many modern roads were originally Indian trails.

As they turned to their left and started north on the trail, they were grateful the Indians had made such a clear path for them, especially as it began winding this way and that. It was a series of switchbacks, zig-zagging up the steep mountainside. About thirty-five minutes later, they saw the next landmark. The map showed a tree with the picture of an arrowhead carved in its trunk, and there it was. They stopped to take a long drink and look around. It was nice to know they were going the right way.

"I wonder how many people have been on this trail since the Indians," said Rachel.

"Maybe hikers or hunters," said Josh. They weren't talking much. The air was getting thinner, and they were breathing more heavily. The trail wound around, and about fifteen minutes later, they reached the next landmark on the map. It was a huge boulder that sparkled in the sun, because of all the quartz in it. It marked the beginning of different terrain. Looking up, there weren't as many trees, and they could clearly see the top of the mountain. There were also more rocks. At the boulder, they were to turn northwest and look for three tall pine trees in a row.

"I'm hungry," said Rachel, plopping down on the ground and removing her backpack.

"Okay," agreed Josh, who removed his backpack, let it drop, and sat down beside it.

Soon they were both chewing and saying, "Mmmm. Tastes good." Josh smiled because Rachel had jelly on her nose.

She knew that smile. "What?"

"Nothing," he shrugged and turned his attention to the map. "Just thinking about the treasure."

They each ate half their sandwich and decided to save the rest for after they found the treasure. Soon, they were on their way again, but the climb was a lot steeper. They moved more slowly, stopping to drink water more often, just as they had been taught. "Look!" shouted Josh, pointing almost due north. Rachel saw the three tall pines, standing like giant guardians. They forgot to keep an easy pace and ran as fast as they could. By the time they reached the three pines, they fell to the ground, gasping for air. They looked up at the blue sky, watching the clouds float by.

When they were breathing normally, they got up to check the map. They turned north, and there it was! The opening of a cave. It was dark and almost covered over by brush. If they hadn't had the map, they would have missed it. They walked to the mouth of the opening and stood, looking into the darkness. "One hundred steps," said Rachel quietly.

"Are you ready?" asked Josh.

"Yeah." They took off their backpacks and put away the compass and map, then pulled away enough brush to enter the cave. The warm sunlight and gentle breeze felt good on their backs. They took one last drink from their water bottles and put them in their backpacks, removing their

flashlights. As they zipped their packs and put their arms through the shoulder straps, they stared at the pitch-black unknown ahead. Josh held out his hand. He had seen the look on his sister's face, like the first time they had ridden the roller coaster with Mom and Dad. Despite the butterflies in his stomach, he knew he was the braver one.

Normally, Rachel would have laughed and shoved Josh's hand away, but not today. She wanted to make sure they didn't get separated in the dark, and of course, she knew her brother needed her to hold his hand. Without her, he would probably run back down the mountain!

"Okay. Here we go," Josh said bravely. They stepped into the cave and turned on their flashlights.

Together, they counted, "One… two… three…." One hundred seemed years away. The walls were close together, which made it easy to follow the path. Why did Grandma and Grandpa tell them to go straight? This was easy. Then, about fifty steps in, they entered a cavern that looked as big as Grandma and Grandpa's log cabin. They stopped and pointed their flashlights in different directions, trying to figure out which way to go, looking for old trunks or anything that might be treasure.

"There's nothing in here," Josh sighed.

Rachel squeezed his hand without realizing it. She whispered, "I know, but we have fifty steps to go. Which way is straight?" They stood quietly, thinking. Then she remembered. "Hey, Grandma said that we'd only need flashlights for *part* of the way."

"She did?"

"Yeah. *Part* of the way. And when I asked her about it, Grandpa wouldn't let her say anything more. I think it's a clue."

"Yeah!" said Josh loudly, and they heard the echo of his voice. "Wow!" they both yelled, waving their flashlights around the cavern, laughing at the repeated echoes of their voices. Josh stopped and put his flashlight under his chin, making the scariest face he could. Rachel yelled and did the same. For a moment, they were totally distracted from thinking about their problem. In such moments, great ideas often come to us.

Rachel stopped. "Hey! If we don't need our flashlights all the time, it means there must be some light in this cave. Let's turn off our flashlights and see if we can see any light."

"Oooooh, right," said Josh. Sure enough, as soon as their flashlights were off, they saw a long, thin, vertical gleam of light straight in front of them. They turned on their flashlights and pointed them to the sides so they could move toward the sliver of light, which became bigger as they drew closer. Fifty steps later, they entered a narrow, zig-zag of a passageway and stumbled into a warmly lit room.

3
BB

The room was about the size of a large bedroom with a very high ceiling. Their eyes were drawn immediately to a large, circular hole above. They had never seen anything like it. The rim was like a rainbow that danced and sparkled, and warm light poured through to illuminate the entire room. "Wow," they murmured. As their eyes adjusted to the light, they heard a trickle of water to their left. Water flowed down a rock wall and formed a pond on the floor below. They turned off their flashlights and walked over to check it out. The water was so clear, they could see themselves in it, but they couldn't tell how deep it was.

"I wonder if this is good to drink?" asked Josh.

"Grrrr!"

A bear! The growl came from across the room, behind them.

Josh pointed to the opening of the passageway, and Rachel nodded. They did what they had been taught to do and moved very slowly and quietly toward the opening of the passageway, but before they could reach it and run, they heard, "Wait!"

The command came from the same place as the growl! They turned, expecting to find a man alongside a bear. Instead, they saw what they had most feared: a rather thin but large black bear. He yawned as he said, "Please excuse me. I didn't mean to startle you. I always growl when I wake up from hibernation."

Stunned in disbelief, the twins watched as the bear stretched and rose to his full height of six feet, yawning again. "Who are you, and how did you get here?"

Completely flabbergasted to be asked a question by a bear, Josh and Rachel stared, not knowing whether to scream, run, or both. The bear came down on all paws and began walking slowly towards them. Josh blurted out, "Uh, we're Josh and Rachel, and..."

"And...and our grandparents gave us a treasure map to get here," answered Rachel.

"Ah. I see." The bear stopped and examined their faces, nodding, as if he recognized them. Then he tilted his head and squinted his eyes, like he was remembering something. The twins were still on their guard, but his deep voice and gentle manner were not frightening at all.

"Um...uh...can I ask...who are you?" Rachel was trying to be brave.

"And how can you talk?" gulped Josh.

The bear laughed a deep, wonderful

laugh. "Humans call me BB, and I have always been able to speak their languages. As you can see, I am not an ordinary black bear."

Of course! BB was short for Black Bear. The twins looked at each other, knowing they were thinking the same thing.

"So tell me, Josh and Rachel, why have you come to my humble abode?"

Josh answered first. "Well, our grandparents gave us a map to this cave… uh…your cave, and they said it would lead us to a treasure."

"That's right," added Rachel. "But – and I don't mean to be disrespectful – looking around your room…um…I don't see anything really valuable." That's when they noticed the large basket in the corner across from a bed of leaves, where the bear had first spoken to them.

"Ahhhh," said BB, as he continued

to stare at them. He moved even closer, and then walked between them toward the pond, his soft fur tickling their arms. They waited as he drank, and between slurps, he explained. "This treasure...cannot be seen with your eyes...or touched with your hands. That is...the treasure your grandparents wish you to find."

"I don't understand," said Josh, irritated. "Why would Grandma and Grandpa send us all this way for nothing?"

"Yes. Why would they call it a treasure hunt if there is nothing to bring back to them?" asked Rachel.

BB shook his head, water flying in all directions, and turned to join them. "Where are my manners? Please sit down. And why don't you have your lunch? I haven't eaten in months, and I'm famished!" The twins sank slowly to the ground as BB lumbered over to the basket. "Ahhhh." With his teeth, he picked up the basket of nuts and dried berries. "I prepared this repast for just this occasion." The twins watched their strange, new friend set the large basket down in front of them, lie down next to it, and begin eating. They were so fascinated by his every movement, they sat like statues, hardly breathing, still holding their flashlights.

After BB had chewed a mouthful and said a few "Mmmmms," he looked at the twins and said, "Well, aren't you hungry? I know your grandmother wouldn't have sent you empty-handed."

He knows Grandma!

They put down their flashlights, shrugged off their backpacks, and removed their water bottles and bag lunches. BB stopped eating and stretched his nose very close to Rachel's face. "I see, you have already eaten some of your sandwich." She froze, looking into his eyes, and BB's tongue licked the dried jelly from her nose.

"Ah!" she instinctively drew back, but at the same time, she was astonished at how sweet BB's breath smelled.

"Excuse me, Rachel. Mmmmm." BB licked his lips. "Jelly is one of my irresistible favorites."

That's when Rachel realized the joke her brother had played on her. She glared at him. "Thanks for telling me!"

Josh laughed. A bear was talking and

had just licked jelly off his sister's nose –
this was the best day ever!

BB offered some of his nuts and
berries in trade for some of their potato
chips and apple pieces. They talked about
what bears like to eat and what humans
like to eat, and what was good for them and
what wasn't. The twins wondered if BB's
mom and dad had taught him things like
that. At the same time, both were thinking,
I'm so glad he's not eating ME!

BB swallowed and said, "That was
good. Isn't it amazing how everything
every species needs is provided to them in
this Earth?" He took the basket in his teeth
and set it aside as the twins put their trash
and water bottles in their backpacks. They
thought, *Don't want to attract bears* – and
then shook their heads considering their
present circumstances.

"Now, let's talk about this treasure you

are looking for. It has a title, you know."

"A title?" The twins said at the same time and laughed. They set their backpacks on either side of them.

"Yes," he said. "The greatest treasure a human being can have is the meaning of life."

"The meaning of life?" Josh was completely disappointed.

"That can be anything!" cried Rachel. "The meaning of life is just an idea. Everyone has their own ideas."

"Explain," commanded BB.

"Some girls spend all their time trying to look prettier, and some boys, all they think about is how they look. People spend all this time trying to eat healthy food and work out so they're strong. I mean, in our city there are like ten gyms and spas and stuff."

"Some people are all about sports or

music or their job," Josh offered. "I guess that's where they find the meaning of their life."

BB cocked his head. "So what you're saying is that humans find the meaning to their lives in their jobs, their hobbies, and their physical appearance?"

Josh's eyes narrowed, which meant he was seeing something and about to tell it. "Yes…and there's also…our family and friends. They're important. Like when my friend Jason's parents took the whole family to see him in a play. Jason said it was so great to hear the applause and know that his family was there. That really meant a lot to him."

BB nodded. "I think I understand. You are saying that relationships with people give meaning to your lives."

"Yes," Josh nodded vigorously. "That's really important to people."

"You have told me a lot of things that can give meaning to your lives. I believe you are right, and these are all good things. But do they last? When you get older, you may not be able to do the things you could do when you were younger. You can't work or do the same sports. Your skin gets wrinkled and your body weaker. Maybe your spouse and the people you love die before you do, or you die and after a while, you are forgotten. What is the meaning of your life then?"

Rachel sighed, and Josh looked down at the ground. Neither one had an answer to that, and it made them feel sad and scared all at the same time.

BB looked like he was pleased, but not in a mean way. It wasn't a "Gotcha!" expression, but more of a now-we-can-know-something-we-have-never-known-before look. "Children, the true meaning of life lasts forever, through every change, even after you die. That's why it is the greatest treasure of all treasures. No matter how old you are, what you look like, what your situation may be – and even after you die – the true meaning of life remains the same. Yesterday, today, and forever."

The twins had heard that phrase, "yesterday, today, and forever," somewhere before, but neither could remember. Josh asked, "Soooo...what always stays the same?" His face revealed that he was very doubtful this would be a treasure he would like.

"With this treasure, no matter what you face, you know what you are going through has meaning. The treasure gives you the courage to face a bully, to help you do hard work in school, to be a good friend, and obey your parents and teachers. Doing the right thing is often very hard, and life is full of problems and hurt, so humans need to know that it's all worth it. The meaning of life shows you that everything you experience is for a good reason, that your lives mean something, even after you die."

BB rose on his four paws, stretching and shaking himself. Even though he was skinny after hibernation, the twins saw how strong he was. As they stood with him, he said, "Humans are fascinating. You can't decide who your mother and father are, where you are born, or many of the circumstances you grow up in; but all along

the way, and certainly when you are older, you decide. You choose who you want to be friends with, whether you want to play basketball or the flute, and eventually what you want to be when you grow up. Tell me, why did you come here?"

"Well, our grandparents sent us," said Josh.

Then Rachel remembered, "But Grandma said we didn't have to go."

"Oh yeah," said Josh. "Ah…I see. You're saying that we chose to come here."

"Exactly!" BB did what could only be called a little dance, and the twins laughed at how silly he looked. They patted him on his back and stroked his soft fur. He closed his eyes and seemed to purr with satisfaction. "Now it is time for you to make your first decision in discovering the treasure and the meaning of life." He turned to his left. There were two doors, one on either side of the pond of water.

"Wait! I don't remember seeing those doors before," said Josh.

"Yeah. Did you just put them there?" Rachel wondered if BB could do magic.

"Remember, I'm not an ordinary black bear, children," BB growled what could only be interpreted as a serious reminder. "Now what is the choice you have to make with these two doors?"

The twin's mouths dropped open as writing appeared on each door. As the water dripped into the pond, they read CURSE on the door to their left and BLESSING on the door to their right.

"The blessing, of course," answered Josh.

"What will happen if we walk through the BLESSING door?" Rachel asked.

"Well, it does say BLESSING!" growled BB, this time like a belly laugh.

Josh was the first to reach the BLESSING door. His father had told him that he was always to open doors for his mother, sister, or any girl. He wasn't sure about bears, but he didn't want to take any chances. He pushed down on the lever, took a deep breath, and pushed the door in. His eyes widened, and Rachel gasped.

4
The Perfect Place

Their first breath filled them with a
peace and joy they had never felt before.
Alive. Free. Strong. Those words couldn't
make anyone understand what they were
experiencing. Their senses were filled with
colors, sounds, and a brightness that made
them feel more at home than any other
place in the world. They began to walk
down a path that put a bounce of joy in
every step. BB followed behind, feeling like
a parent who was watching their children

open a present they had always wanted.

"Where are we?" Josh called back.

"Where do you think we are?" BB replied.

"Oh BB! This is a beautiful, perfect place," answered Rachel.

They proceeded on the path. Soon they came upon a stream that shone in multiple shades of blue. BB stopped to drink, so the twins knelt, dipped their hands in the cool water, and drank. They giggled. It was like they had never tasted real water before. They got up and followed BB on the path, marveling at the magnificent trees and the flowers that hummed in a multitude of colors. All kinds of animals let them touch them and pet them. There was no fear in them or the children. The little animals were not even afraid of BB! They all seemed glad to see him, scampering around his feet, making happy sounds when he nudged them, and then running off.

BB stopped when they came to a large, grassy clearing. The twins stood on either side of him. "What do you see, children?"

Almost in unison, the twins pointed, "The two trees." The trees were about twenty feet from each other, one just to the left of the center of the round circle of lush grass, the other to the right, about ten feet from the edge of the clearing. Each had delicious-looking fruit growing on it, but not like any fruit they had seen.

"The tree to your left is called the Tree of Life," BB explained. "The tree to your right is called the Tree of the Knowledge of Good and Evil. You are about to witness the first significant event in human history. No one can see you or hear you, but be silent. Watch. Listen."

Before they saw them, they heard them laughing in the wooded area on the other side of the clearing. Soon, a man and a woman walked hand-in-hand into the clearing and stopped. The twins leaned forward and stared at them. They had never seen such beautiful people. They were so perfect, but it was more than that. They were pure goodness, and the children immediately loved them. They felt close to them. Rachel noticed their clothes. What were they made of? The material glistened like light, but you couldn't see through it. She wanted to ask BB, but he had told them to be quiet.

The man said something to the woman, and she smiled and began to respond, but she was interrupted by the sound of a wonderful melody coming from the side of the clearing where the Tree of the Knowledge of Good and Evil stood. The man and woman turned, as did the children, and watched a magnificent creature enter the clearing. It looked like a beautifully colored snake – but stood upright, with arms and legs – and took several steps toward the tree. It continued to hum and smile at the man and woman. The woman dropped the man's hand and walked slowly toward the creature and the tree. The man watched her go then turned to tend to something in the brush.

Did the man and woman know this creature? It folded its arms and said to the woman, "Did God really say you couldn't eat of all the trees in this garden?" It talked! The twins' eyes grew bigger, but they weren't too shocked. After all, they had been talking to a bear!

The woman answered, "God told us we can eat of every tree except this one. We can't touch it or eat its fruit, or we will die."

The creature threw back its head and laughed. "You won't die! God knows that when you eat of this tree, you will be like him. You will know what is good and what is evil, just like he knows. Surely, he wants you to know everything."

The woman studied the Tree of the Knowledge of Good and Evil. The twins didn't know how, but they knew what the woman was thinking as she studied the tree. To her, it looked delicious. To her, it looked like a good fruit that would make her wise like God. But in their hearts, they knew it wasn't anything like that! The twins knew that something terrible would happen if she ate it.

The woman reached up and picked a piece of fruit. Inside, the children were crying out, "Don't eat it! Please don't eat it!" They saw the man turn toward her and watch as she took a bite of the fruit.

The creature smiled broadly as the woman chewed and swallowed – and then picked another piece of fruit, walked over to the man, and gave it to him. He gazed at the fruit in his hand.

Oh no! He took a bite too!

And that's when it happened. As soon as the man swallowed his first bite, everything changed. The man and woman's beautiful clothes began to melt away, and BB let out a low growl so that the twins only saw the man and woman's faces, humiliated with shame. But the twins knew the man and woman were naked as they ran into the woods. Josh and Rachel could hear them tearing at leaves as they tried to cover themselves.

The twins looked at the creature. He had the most wicked grin, and he began humming that tune again. Even now, the music was so beautiful! Suddenly his tongue shot out of his mouth, wiggled back and forth, and slid back in. The twins shuddered, and each thought, *It's beautiful on the outside, but evil through and through.* Then the creature saw something that caused it to stop humming and freeze in terror.

Josh and Rachel turned to see another man, standing by the other tree, the Tree of Life. They had never seen anyone like him. He wore clothes like the man and woman had worn before they ate the fruit, but there was a wide, golden belt around his waist. His hair and beard were white as snow, and his eyes were glowing with life. He was surely the Lord of this place! He turned from the creature to the woods, where the man and woman had fled. "Adam! Adam! Where are you?" His words felt like mighty waves of water moving over them and through them.

Josh and Rachel looked at each other. Of course! They had heard about this in Sunday school. This was the Garden of Eden, the man and the woman were Adam and Eve, and the creature was the devil. Adam and Eve slowly walked out of the woods, covered with leaves. They weren't laughing or holding hands now. Their shoulders slumped, and they looked down at the ground. Adam mumbled, "I heard you coming and hid. I was afraid because I was naked."

The Lord of the Garden asked him, "Who told you that you were naked? Did you

eat of that tree?" and he pointed to the Tree of the Knowledge of Good and Evil.

Then Adam did something the twins could not believe. He stood tall and glared at the Lord, "The woman you gave me handed me the fruit, and I ate it!"

That was an attitude Josh and Rachel's parents never tolerated! But the Lord simply turned to the woman and asked kindly, "Eve, what did you do?"

The look on Eve's face! Her attitude was as bad as Adam's. "The serpent lied to me and I believed him! That's why I ate the fruit."

The scene froze.

BB said, "Tell me what you see, children."

"Everything's ruined," Josh blurted out.

"They don't even look the same. They were so awesome before!" cried Rachel.

BB tilted his head. "God warned them that if they ate of the Tree of the Knowledge of Good and Evil, they would die, but did they die? Look. They are still alive."

The twins stared at Adam and Eve, covered with leaves, angry and bitter. Josh shook his head. "Not like they were, though."

Rachel sighed. "Yeah, compared to before, it's like they're dead inside."

"Ah! You have seen the truth! They have lost the meaning of life."

"Is the Lord going to punish them? What's going to happen to them?" asked Josh.

"Watch." BB turned back to the scene.

The Lord whistled, and the cutest lamb trotted out of the woods and right to him. Its wool was white and soft, and the children wished they could run over and pet it. The Lord knelt, stroked it, and they could not see what he was doing. They only saw the lamb sink to the ground, lifeless, and Adam and Eve cry out in anguish. The Lord gently put his hands on the lamb and spoke something. He arose with only the lambskin in his hands. The lamb was gone, but they saw a puddle of blood where it had been.

The Lord had tears in his eyes as he said something. Then he blew on the lambskin, which he began to shape into clothes for Adam and Eve. As the Lord lovingly dressed them, the leaves that had covered them dropped to the ground and were already turning brown. Adam and Eve were still weeping over the slain lamb. They had never seen anything die.

BB nuzzled Rachel and then Josh, as tears coursed down their cheeks. "I know this is hard to understand, but what the Lord did was right and good. Even after they disobeyed him, he loved Adam and Eve. He didn't want them to be naked and cold. He sacrificed the lamb to save his beloved children. Do you see?"

The twins were still sad but felt better. They watched the Lord walk over to the creature. He said, "Because you have led humans to sin against God, you will crawl on your belly as more cursed than any other creature." The serpent's arms and legs faded away as it fell to the ground with a hiss. The Lord looked down at the creature and continued, "There will be war between you and the woman, but a woman will give birth to a man whose father is not a man. God will be his father. You will hurt him for a time, but he will crush you forever." The serpent slithered to the edge of the clearing and out of sight, but the evil presence of the creature was still there, watching, listening.

The Lord turned around and walked to Adam and Eve. "You are in a terrible condition, and I don't want you to eat of the Tree of Life, which would seal you in sin, with no way back to me forever. So, I am expelling you from the Garden." BB nudged the children to stand at the side of the path. The Lord led Adam and Eve toward it. After they had passed, BB nudged the twins to follow.

How changed was the walk out from the walk in! A great sadness filled their hearts. As they exited the Garden, the Lord waved his right hand, and two powerful angels with wings appeared. They stood at the entrance to the Garden with a flaming sword. Then the children were standing with BB in his cave.

5
The Heart of the Matter

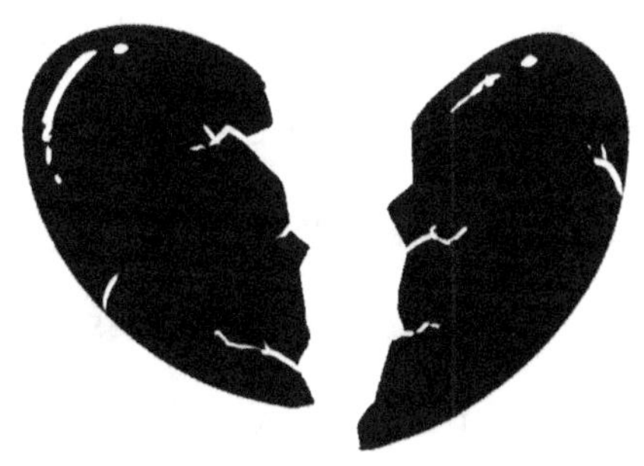

Josh was angry. "Is this the treasure? This is awful! This is no treasure."

"Don't be disrespectful, Josh," said Rachel. "But BB, please tell us this is not the treasure."

"Tell me, children, what caused everything to change from good to bad?"

"Eating the fruit of the bad tree," said Rachel.

"No, it was because they disobeyed God," Josh said bitterly.

"You are right, Josh." BB was

thoughtful. "There is something you need to know about God. When he commands you not to do something, it is because he loves you and doesn't want you to be hurt or get into trouble, just like all the adults who love you. They give you rules because they care about you. God gives you rules to keep you safe, and obeying them brings good things into your life. On the other hand, the creature – Satan – is evil and will always try to get you to be disrespectful and break God's rules. He wants to ruin your life, even kill you if he can."

BB stopped and looked from one twin to the other. "Did you notice? No one changed when Eve ate. They only changed after Adam ate. Why?"

"Mom told me it was because Eve was...de...deceived. She says being deceived means believing lies," answered Rachel.

"Your mother is wise," said BB. "The

serpent led Eve to believe the lie that God wanted her to disobey him, that he really didn't mean what he said. She believed that lie. She was deceived into thinking she was doing what God wanted her to do. But Adam knew the truth. He knew God meant what he said. That's why God held the man responsible for sin, so it is through the man that sin passes to the children."

"So Adam messed all of us up!" Josh shook his head and threw up his hands. He started to walk away, and Rachel thought, *There he goes, off to pout.*

BB gently butted Josh's chest with his nose, causing him to stand still and look right into BB's eyes. "One decision, Josh. Two trees. God gave humans the right to choose. It shows that he respects you." Then BB looked to Rachel, who nodded. BB backed away a little. "One decision made everything go wrong, so… God will offer one decision to put everything right."

Josh was curious. "BB, was the Lord of the Garden...God?"

"Yes, the Lord God. You saw that he was a little different from Adam and Eve, didn't you?" The twins nodded. "You know, God is three persons in one, which is hard to understand. They are kind of like the apple you had for lunch. There's the core, the meat, and the skin. Each part has a purpose, but they are one as the apple core, the apple meat, and the apple skin; like God the Father, God the Son, and God the Holy Spirit."

"My friend Charlie eats the whole apple, core and all!" cried Josh.

"Oooooh. I forgot. Yuck," said Rachel.

"Well, Charlie found goodness in all of it, didn't he? And that's just like God. There's the Father, the Son, and the Holy Spirit, and they are all good. They think and act alike even though they have different jobs. They agree on everything and always do what is right. In the beginning, the Lord God talked with Adam and Eve in the Garden and gave humans their eternal value and purpose."

"What do you mean, eternal value and purpose?" asked Rachel.

BB flopped on the ground as only a bear can flop. The twins wanted to pet him, but they had to sit in front of him to be polite and listen. Each sat cross-legged, leaning toward him.

"Some scientists and many teachers will tell you that you were not created by God. They say there was a big bang in the universe that formed the Earth, which just happened to contain living cells that changed and evolved...."

"Oh! I know! Evolution. Dad says that some of it is right and some of it is wrong, that...," Josh's voice began to mimic his dad, "the part about fruit flies changing is one thing, but human beings are another. We didn't crawl out of the swamp as a lizard, gradually turn into a monkey, and finally become human beings. We're not robotic mutants, you know!'"

Rachel and BB laughed, and Josh was quite pleased with his impersonation – especially that he remembered all the words!

"If you simply evolved from some kind of ooze, an accident of nature, does that make you feel special?" asked BB.

Rachel shook her head. "No. If that's true, then I'm just...well... a robotic mutant." She giggled because the words sounded so funny.

BB smiled (and it is nearly shocking to see a bear smile). "The Bible tells us that

God created Adam and Eve in his image and likeness, like you are in your father and mother's image and likeness. Tell me, who makes you feel special and loved?"

"Mom and Dad," answered Josh.

"And Grandma and Grandpa, and our friends and family," added Rachel.

"God loved Adam and Eve. They were his family. Everything he had was theirs. Everything he had created was for them. He spent time with them every day and talked with them, just like your parents do with you. Do you see how God gave them eternal value, how he showed them they were special?" The twins nodded. "But that's not all."

BB pulled his basket of nuts and dried fruit closer. "I'm hungry again. It's been a long winter!" He gestured with his nose that they could join him in his snack. "Not only does God give human beings value by loving them, he also gives them purpose. He says, 'Come work with me!'"

"Like making them to be a preacher or doctor or something?" Rachel asked.

"Yes, but it's more than that. You work with him and for him doing the three things he commanded Adam and Eve and all humans to do: Be fruitful and multiply, have dominion over the Earth, and guard and keep the Garden. Now tell me, how are you going to be fruitful and multiply?"

The twins laughed. "I don't know! Get

married and have babies, I guess," giggled Rachel.

"I'm sure your parents want each of you to get married and have children, but if that's the only thing you're going to do, why do they send you to school?"

Josh had an idea. "Well, maybe it's to learn how to be fruitful and multiply in a business or on a farm. In the spring, when we plant one seed in our garden, a whole bunch of carrots or beans grow out of it. Isn't that multiplying?"

"Yes! God loves abundance. He wants lots of children and wants to bless them with lots of everything. He's creative, and he made humans to be creative like him, to do something well so that other people's lives are better. Then those people want to do something well to make other people's lives better, and so on. The key is to discover the things God wants to do with you. Those are your adventures in life! Now, what about having dominion? What do you think that means?"

The twins' faces went blank. BB popped some fruit in his mouth and chewed. "Dominion means rule. God owns the Earth, but he made humans rulers over it. Kangaroos and cheetahs don't rule the Earth. People do. You are to take good care of it and all the living creatures – especially me!" He threw his head around and opened his mouth, and the twins convulsed with laughter as they tried to throw berries and nuts in his mouth. Finally, BB had a good mouthful and was contentedly chewing. "Thank you," he swallowed. "The last thing God commanded Adam and Eve to do was to keep and guard the Garden. Now tell me, if you must guard something, if you have to hold onto something and keep it, what does that mean?"

"Someone wants to take it from you!" cried Josh.

Rachel shut her eyes and grimaced. "Adam and Eve let the devil in."

BB looked pleased and nodded. "Satan means adversary. He opposes God and wants to destroy everyone and everything God loves. He has a dark magic, you know, so he took the form of a serpent. We know this because the Bible tells us that Satan is sometimes called a serpent. I'm very glad God did not call him a bear!"

The twins laughed and said together, "Me too!"

Rachel became very serious. "So…if God gave Adam and Eve their eternal value and purpose before they sinned, did they still have it after they sinned? They were so different."

"Excellent question!" BB cracked another nut in his teeth. The twins watched as he skillfully spit out the shell and chewed the nut. "There is one thing you should always remember: God never lies, and he keeps his word. When he tells you something, you can believe it. So yes, Adam and Eve's – and all human beings' – value and purpose remained after they sinned. But remember: Adam and Eve changed, and so all humans born after them do not know God like Adam and Eve did in the beginning. Your ability to know your value and carry out your purpose suffers because you are now separated from God because of sin. He didn't change. You did."

"What happened to us?" asked Rachel. "I mean, I saw how Adam and Eve changed, but they didn't die. If God doesn't lie, why didn't they die like he said they would?"

"That, dear one, goes to the heart of the matter." BB swallowed another piece of dried fruit. "Tell me, who is the real you?"

Josh sat up straight. "Just ask me! I can tell you who she really is."

"Be quiet, Josh. You don't know everything about me," Rachel glared at him.

BB took another mouthful of berries from the basket and said (because, in case you wondered, bears don't have table manners and can talk and chew at the same time), "Okay, Josh. Tell me, who is the real Rachel?"

Josh frowned. He didn't want to say anything bad about his sister, but he didn't want to just tell the good things either. And what if there were things he didn't know? Suddenly, he realized he had put himself in an impossible situation. He could hear his mother saying, "You might as well come clean and tell the truth, 'cause God knows anyway."

"Josh?" asked BB.

"Well, sometimes Rachel does good things and sometimes she does bad things."

"And I suppose you're good all the time?" said Rachel.

"No, I'm not saying that. Everybody's good sometimes and bad sometimes."

"What you have described, Josh, is the sin nature. You know what is good but still want to sin. We will look more closely at that problem later. But who is the Rachel who causes her to act, to speak?" The twins were a blank again. "Children, each of you, take a walnut out of my basket. Is that the real walnut? Will you just pop it in your mouth?"

"No!" grinned the twins. Then Josh said, "That's the shell. You have to crack it to get to the real nut, which is inside." He grabbed his flashlight and proceeded to crack the shell by hitting it. Then he picked out the nut from inside.

"Exactly. Your physical body, your outer shell, is not the real you. The real you is on the inside, moving your mouth to speak, causing your arms and legs to move. The Bible calls the real you a spirit. When your physical body dies, your spirit will live forever."

BB jumped up on his hind legs and began to dance like the dancing bears in the circus. The twins laughed and jumped up to dance with him. When he suddenly stopped and came down on all paws, they stopped too. "What made you leap up and begin dancing?" he asked.

Rachel answered, "You did!"

"Yeah, we wanted to dance with you," said Josh.

"So, did I make the decision for you?" asked BB.

"Oh...I see. You want us to see how

everything we do is our choice, like with the two trees," said Josh.

"Yes! But now I want you to tell me *who* made that decision. *Who* is the *you* that decided to dance with me? Did your legs decide?"

"No!" Rachel and Josh laughed.

BB chuckled, "Or did you, a spirit inside your body, decide? You are a spirit inside a body, you could say, like a nut inside a shell–"

At this, the twins roared with laughter. "We are all nuts! Ha! Ha!"

His head bobbed up and down, then he continued, "But your spirit is more like the air inside a balloon. If the air goes out of the balloon, it falls to the ground, lifeless. Your spirit is what gives life to your body and exists forever."

Rachel was the first to speak. "So, you're saying that everything I decide comes from inside, that I'm a spirit in a body?"

"Yes. The heart of the matter!" said BB. "Unfortunately, every spirit born of Adam and Eve is born with the desire to sin. So what do you do? You try to be good, but you still want to do bad things."

"Oh," Rachel frowned. "You mean that's why I have such a hard time controlling my temper and keep doing the things I know aren't right?"

"Yes, Rachel." BB shook his head sadly. "Every human is born that way."

"This is deep stuff, BB." Josh closed his eyes. He thought about how Rachel had been honest about her sin. He should be too. He took a deep breath. "Dad is always telling me to stop feeling sorry for myself when I don't get my way. I get so mad! I don't want to talk to anyone."

"That's what sin does, Josh. Sin makes you feel alone. You against everyone else. Now tell me, what do you think is the greatest treasure a human could be given?"

"To go back to being like Adam and Eve before they ate –"

"Yes!" Rachel interrupted. "Before the snake!"

"Ah…yes." BB growled, and the cave disappeared.

6
The War

The twins were standing on a street of gold, so shiny and clear they could almost see through it. They must be in Heaven! BB was standing behind them. They looked around. Everything was awesome! It was so much like the Garden of Eden. The blue sky, the bright light, and the green, green grass. Perfect. But then they realized, there were no people. Before they could ask why, BB said, "Shhhh. Only God knows you're here."

Three angels appeared. They were very tall and majestic, but each was unique. Josh noticed that the one on the left wasn't as muscular as the one on the right, who looked like a warrior. The one in the middle could only be described as a being they could never have imagined. He was covered with sparkling jewels of all colors. There were musical instruments in his chest, and awesome music poured out of his mouth. The twins had to force themselves not to sing along. The music reached into their innermost being and opened their hearts to the greatest love they had ever known.

BB said, "The archangel to your left is Gabriel. He is God's chief messenger. The archangel to your right is Michael, God's chief warrior. And the archangel in the middle is Lucifer, God's light bearer, who inspires worship and praise to God." The three archangels' hands were raised in worship, and all the angels of Heaven appeared and joined them. Josh and Rachel thought their hearts would burst with joy.

Then Lucifer stopped the music. He had a strange expression on his face, took a deep breath, and began to sing a different song... by himself. As he sang, he rose, until he was above all the angels. As he rose and sang, his expression grew darker and more sinister. The twins were filled with dread.

What is he doing? they thought.

He sang out proudly, "I will rise to Heaven! I will raise my throne above the stars of God! I will sit at the top of the mountain of God, on his throne! I will ascend above the heights of the clouds! I will make myself like the Most High!"

As the twins looked in horror, Lucifer sang the same song again and again – and soon it looked like a third of the angels began to sing it and rise to join him! Did they see how they were changing? Just like Lucifer, they transformed from being glorious to a dreadful darkness.

The twins' attention was caught by the appearance of the Lord God. His eyes were filled with fire, but his expression was one of grief. Gabriel put a glistening shofar to his lips and trumpeted a sound of war, cutting through Lucifer's song, but the dark angels sang even louder. The look on their faces! The twins had never seen such wicked defiance. They wondered, *What are they protesting? Heaven?!!!*

Michael raised a flaming sword, and all the angels who had not followed Lucifer began singing praises to the Most High God. Their song of praise grew louder as they followed Michael into the most violent battle the twins had ever witnessed. The dark angels were hatred personified, their eyes pure murder. But the glorious angels, even though they fought fiercely, had that same expression of grief the Lord God had...grief and determination.

Then suddenly, it was over. All battle ceased and all eyes were on the Lord God, who had risen to confront Lucifer. He declared, "I created you in perfection and beauty! I gave you a cherished place in my kingdom! But you have turned to worship yourself instead of me, and every thought and desire of your heart is evil! So I cast you and those who have chosen evil instead of good out of Heaven!"

They saw Lucifer, now the prince of darkness, begin to plummet like a fallen star to the Earth below. He took the form of a dragon, and his massive tail swung around to capture the angels of darkness who followed him. Like a bolt of lightning, he hit the Earth below.

BB growled, and they were standing in his sunlit cave again.

"Wow!" cried Josh.

"What was that?" asked Rachel.

"Children, you have just witnessed the first sin and the origin of evil."

"I thought Adam and Eve were the first to sin," said Rachel.

"Many do, but no. Lucifer chose to believe what he wanted to believe instead of God's truth. He believed his own lie: I don't need God. I'm beautiful and talented and wealthy. I have everything I need in myself. I will kick God off the throne and take his place." The children laughed, as BB spoke in a whiny, snobbish voice and plopped down next to his basket like a spoiled brat. The twins sat to face him.

"I can't believe all those angels went with him," said Josh.

"Well, he had beauty and riches, and his music was captivating," said BB. "So some of the angels got caught up in him and chose to believe his lies. They began to worship and serve him, believing the lie that it was better for them instead of worshiping God." BB sighed a deep sigh. "Satan began the war between himself and God, and all wars between people are a continuation of this war. It is the war between darkness and light that shakes your world today."

"My teacher said that World War II started because Hitler wanted the whole world to bow down to him," offered Josh.

"Where do you think Hitler got that idea?" asked BB.

Josh smiled and nodded. "Satan."

BB shook his head. "Everything wrong with human beings can be found in the song you heard Lucifer sing when he started the war with God. Now, as Satan, he and God fight over the hearts and minds of people, but they fight very differently. God is good, and he brings people to him through his goodness. Satan is evil, and he deceives people into serving him. Always remember: Satan is a liar, and his lies will put you in chains; God tells the truth, and his truth sets you free. That's why the Bible is so important. It is the book of the Truth, because it is the only book God wrote. He wrote it to tell you about the treasure and the meaning of life."

"Like the map?" asked Rachel.

"Ahhhh. The Bible is a human's map for life. God's words tell you where to find the treasure so you can know the meaning of life."

"Wait a minute. Don't other religious books do that too?" asked Josh.

"No, children. The books of other religions or philosophies don't even come close to the Bible, because the Bible was miraculously written by God himself. He chose forty people, over the course of thousands of years, living in different times and places, to write the same story, using the same symbols and expressing the same truths. That's a miracle! You and Rachel live in the same time and place, but don't you see things differently?"

"That's for sure!" cried Rachel, and they both nodded.

"It's called continuity, and continuity is one reason we know God wrote the Bible; but there is another reason. What if I gave you a book, written a hundred years ago, and 90 percent of it told everything that had happened in your lives so far? Would you be interested to know what else it had to say about you?"

"Sure!"

"That's what the Bible does for humans. Today, almost 90 percent of human history has happened exactly as the Bible predicted, sometimes hundreds or thousands of years before it happened. God wants you to know that he wrote the Bible, and he wrote the truth. The Bible is amazing! It tells you the truth about you, about God, the angels, about the devil – and how to win the war with him. Personally, I have a special affection for the Bible, because God named me after it."

The twins were dumbfounded. "Isn't your name Black Bear?" asked Josh.

"Bible Bear," growled BB gently. "But BB is...more...what do kids say? Hip?"

Josh laughed and grabbed a nut to crack. Rachel cocked her head. "Okay, Bible Bear, um...when Josh and I fight...are we letting Satan win the war?"

"What do you and Josh usually fight about?" he asked.

The twins looked at each other. "Well, most of the time it's stupid stuff, but I get really mad when Josh thinks he can tell me what to do because he's a boy."

"Yeah, but you think you know more than me, that you're smarter than me," countered Josh.

"Ahhhh. Tell me, whenever you fight, who are you concerned about?" asked BB.

The twins frowned, and almost at the same time said, "Me."

"Me! Me! Me! Me!" sang BB, dancing around on his hind legs and pounding his chest. "I'm the greatest! I'm the best ever! No one better than me! Me! Me! Me! Me!" The twins jumped up and joined in. After a while, BB stopped, came down on all four paws, and looked them in the eyes. "Does that remind you of anyone?"

"Lucifer...or Satan now," said Josh.

"Oh, I get it!" said Rachel. "That's what he did in the Garden! He got Adam and Eve to think about themselves instead of God, just like he did with the dark angels. And he was singing that song, the same song we heard in the Garden!"

"Rachel, you have just described what started the war and the root of all sin: selfishness and self-centeredness. In case you didn't know, you and Josh and every baby are born believing you are the center of the universe instead of God. You want to tell others what to do and prove you're smarter than everyone else (*did he just wink at them?*) – and you don't care who you hurt or what it costs to get what you want. So you say and do terrible things, and then you make excuses or blame others when you are caught. That's sin!"

The twins frowned.

"Sin is selfish and evil and cruel, the root of all problems with humans. Alas," BB sighed, "sin separates people from God, so sin is God's problem too."

"Why is it God's problem?" asked Josh.

"Because God loves humans!" BB began to tickle the twins with his nose, and they tried running away, but he kept catching them. "He misses what it was like in the Garden of Eden, when they could talk and play and laugh together." Finally, he sauntered over to the pool of water to get a long drink. The twins got their water bottles and filled them from the pool, listening to BB slurp and slurp. When he finished, he licked his lips and plopped on the floor next to his basket, which was only half full now. The twins sat down with him.

"God never wanted humans to be away from him, to have fights and wars, or to get sick and die. All of that is because Adam obeyed Satan instead of God. Satan captured humans, so God had a plan to win the war and get you back."

"I want to know that plan!" said Josh.

"Well, do you remember what He told Satan, after Adam and Eve sinned?"

"He said girls would be afraid of snakes," said Josh, a little too triumphantly.

Rachel shuddered. "Yes, but he also said a woman would have a son who…

who…I forget….”

"A woman would have a son whose father would not be a man. It is the first prophecy in the Bible about Jesus of Nazareth. His father would be God, so Jesus would not be born a sinful man. If God was not Jesus' father, there is no treasure."

"Why?" asked Rachel.

BB swallowed a mouthful of berries. "Do you remember the lamb in the Garden?" The children's faces fell, remembering how it had to die to make clothes for Adam and Eve. "The Lord was showing Adam and Eve and all humans that only the blood of an innocent, sinless lamb – a man who had never sinned – could pay for Adam's sin. One sinless man had to pay for Adam's sin and the sins of all people. That lamb was Jesus of Nazareth. God the Father was his father, so he was born without sin."

"But did Jesus never sin?" asked Rachel.

"Jesus was tempted by Satan in every way a human is tempted, but unlike Adam, Jesus made the decision not to sin. He stayed innocent, so he could die for the guilty. And, he showed you how to defeat Satan."

"How did he do that?" asked Josh.

"He used the sword of the Spirit."

"A sword?" Josh loved swords and sword fights!

"The words of God in the Bible are called the sword of the Spirit. Satan hates God's words and runs away when you use the sword of the Spirit. When Satan tempts you to sin or tries to deceive you with a lie, you speak God's words from the Bible – the Truth – and watch him run!"

"Wow! I like that!" Then Josh paused and looked down. "BB, I'm still not sure if I understand why Jesus had to never commit a sin. Couldn't he just die for us?" asked

Josh.

"I want to know why he had to die," added Rachel.

BB was quiet a moment. "Let's say you both steal candy from the store, and your parents tell you that the consequence is being grounded for a month. Josh, can you do Rachel's punishment?"

"Why would I want to do that?" Josh looked confused.

"Just think about it. If both you and Rachel have sinned, who could come forward and pay for your sins? Wouldn't it have to be someone who hadn't sinned?"

"Oh…I see!" said Rachel. "Someone without sin is the only one who could pay for those who have sinned."

"But there is a deeper truth here. I don't know if you can handle it yet. It has to do with blood."

"Ooooh. Just try! Please tell us!" cried

the twins. They had never had a problem with blood and found it quite fascinating.

BB paused a moment. "The Bible says that life, the life of every creature, is in their blood. Look at all the veins in your arms and hands. Your blood flows throughout your body and gives it life. Blood represents life. Understand?"

The twins nodded.

"Adam's sin robbed God of the lives of his children, so one man's life – the sinless blood of Jesus – was sacrificed to bring you back to the Father."

"I think I understand," said Rachel. "Jesus' sinless blood paid for our sin...."

"Oh!" cried Josh. "Jesus shed his blood, so our spirits can be alive and know God again..."

"So we can be with God like Adam and Eve were!" said Rachel.

"Yes! Jesus's blood paid for your sins,

defeated the devil, and made a way home to the Father. Jesus is the Lamb of God, who takes away the sin of the world."

Before the twins could ask another question, BB growled, and the cave vanished.

7
The Lamb

They stood on the bank of a river, surrounded by a great crowd of people. A wild-looking man was walking into the river, and the twins marveled at his long, black hair and strange clothes. He wore a camel's hair tunic with a leather belt, and it was strange to see him clothed like that and step into the deeper water. *Why didn't he have a bathing suit on?*

He cried out, "Repent, for the day of

the Lord is at hand!"

People followed him into the water to be immersed, one after another, all of them in their clothes! Suddenly, the wild man stopped and looked toward the shore, about twenty feet from where BB and the twins stood. They turned to follow his gaze, and he cried, "Behold the Lamb of God, who takes away the sin of the world!"

They knew the man was Jesus, but he didn't look like any of the pictures they had seen in church. He was kind of tall, had sandy-brown hair, and his eyes were a wondrous color filled with love. He stepped into the river, walking toward the wild man, who said, "I'm not worthy to baptize you. You should baptize me."

"Baptize me. It is the right thing to do," Jesus said.

So the wild man (the twins now understood he was John the Baptist) put Jesus under the water and brought him back up again. Jesus walked out of the water, stepped onto the bank, and a shimmering light enveloped him. It looked a lot like Adam and Eve's clothes in the Garden of Eden. At the same time, from the skies above came a deep voice, "This is my beloved Son, in whom I am well pleased!"

BB growled, and they stood on a green, grassy hillside, looking down on a sparkling sea. He said, "This is the Sea of Galilee." A huge crowd of people surrounded them, covering the hillside, but no one said, "Sit down, I can't see," or "Help! A bear!" or anything like that. The twins knew no one could see them but Jesus, who sat on the hilltop, speaking the most wonderful words. They didn't understand everything he said, and some of it was upsetting, but they sensed every word was true and wise.

He said they were salt and light to

the world, and he was the fulfillment of all the Law and Prophets. He said that if you thought a lot about how angry you were with someone, if you just *thought* about it a lot, then you had murdered them in your heart! Not only that, he said to love and pray for your enemies! The twins looked at each other, thinking of the bully in their school. That's impossible!

He said that when you pray and do good deeds, do it for God and not to draw attention to yourself. He said to forgive everyone, or God wouldn't forgive you!

And he talked a lot about money, that you shouldn't love money but love God, that God would see that you had what you need if you trust him. He said, "Treat others the way you want to be treated." The Golden Rule! The twins knew that one. They heard it all the time from their parents and grandparents.

Jesus talked about how narrow the road of salvation was, and how wide the road to destruction was. That was scary, but the way he said it was comforting, like that narrow road was as obvious as the yellow brick road in *The Wizard of Oz.* He said there were a lot of false prophets and teachers telling lies, who would act like your friend and seem good, but they would do wicked things. And he ended by saying that anyone who built their house on his words would stand through any storm, but those who built their houses on the lies of the enemy would fall apart when the storm hit.

There was such a presence of peace and joy around Jesus, the twins wanted to listen to him forever. They were disappointed when he stopped speaking and began to walk through the crowd, down the hillside. He hugged people and smiled a lot, taking time to talk to them along the way. He even crouched down to talk to the little children, and when he passed the twins and BB, they thought he looked right at them. *Did he see them and smile?*

Their hands rested upon BB's back as they followed closely behind Jesus. His disciples were such a happy group of men and women, chattering about what they had just heard, some talking with him. A couple of times, he threw his head back and laughed. And what a laugh! It thrilled their hearts, and BB bobbed his head up and down.

The walk was wonderful until they saw a hideous looking man coming toward them. He was dressed in rags, and the smell was terrible. There were boil-like sores covering his hands, arms, feet, and face, and some of his fingers and toes were missing. The twins covered their mouths and noses as the man painfully bowed before Jesus and said, "Please, Lord, I know you can make me clean, if you want to."

Jesus said, "I want to," and touched the man, right on his sores!

Immediately, the sores disappeared, his fingers were all there, and the smell was gone. The man was about to shout – there was such joy on his face – but Jesus stopped him and told him to go to the priest in the synagogue and show him that he was clean. The man hurried away, his hands lifted up, trying not to be too loud in thanking and praising God.

They continued to follow Jesus as he entered the city of Capernaum. Again, his disciples talked about what had just happened, and Jesus smiled and answered their questions. He put his arm around one as they walked and talked. Then a man in a Roman soldier's uniform approached Jesus. He looked very important in his glistening helmet with the tall plume, and he had an imposing sword on his wide belt. He said, "Lord, I beg you to come heal my servant, who is at my home, dying."

Jesus said, "Of course, I will come and heal him."

But the soldier put out his hand to stop him. "My house is not worthy of you, so just say the word from here. I know the authority you have, and all you need to do is say the word and my servant will be healed."

Then the twins saw a look on Jesus'

face they had never seen: amazement! He was completely astonished at this man. "You have greater faith in me than anyone else I have met, and you are not even a Jew! Go home. Your servant is healed." The man thanked Jesus with a big smile and turned to leave.

Soon, Jesus and his followers reached the seashore, where they all got in a boat. Oh no! The twins remembered this from Sunday school. They held tightly onto BB after they had settled down in the stern of the boat, near Jesus, who grabbed a pillow and promptly fell asleep. Sure enough, when they were in the middle of the Sea of Galilee, a terrible storm arose, tossing the boat like it was made of toothpicks. Waves began washing over the side, drenching them in the cold water, and the twins buried their heads in BB's fur.

They heard a couple of the disciples

awaken Jesus with, "Master! Don't you care that we are going to die?"

Peeking through BB's fur, the twins saw Jesus sit up and look at his disciples. They could tell he was disappointed. The twins thought, *I don't want him to ever look at me that way!*

"Why are you afraid?" he asked, shaking his head. "You have little faith." Then he stood and commanded, "Peace! Be still!" Immediately, the wind and the waves were calm again.

The men who had awakened Jesus returned to their places on the boat, and one said to the other, "Did you see that? Even the wind and waves obey him."

The rest of the voyage was sunny and warm, and they soon landed on the other shore. That's when the real excitement began. They had hardly left the boat when a man, if you could call him that, streaked toward them, screaming like a wild animal and almost naked! He waved his fists like he wanted to kill them, foaming at the mouth and smelling like the outhouses at their summer camp. He had cuts all over his body, and on his wrists and ankles he dragged chains that had obviously not held him.

They were shocked when the man suddenly fell before Jesus, who said, "Come out of him, you unclean spirit."

The man cried out, "What business do you have with me, Jesus, Son of the Most High God? I implore you by God, do not torment me!"

Jesus asked, "What is your name?"

Now he spoke in a different, very raspy voice, "My name is Legion, for we are many. Please, send us into the pigs on the mountainside."

"Go then," commanded Jesus. And

the man who had been possessed of many demons was completely transformed. His face looked like he had just awakened from the worst nightmare. He smiled, rose to his feet, and immediately went to wash himself in the water. The disciples gave him clothes to wear, food and drink, and as they were helping him, the twins heard squeals coming from the mountainside. They looked up and watched a herd of crazed pigs run over a cliff into the sea below.

Their attention returned to the changed man, who was thanking Jesus again and again, weeping and saying that he never wanted to leave him. Jesus embraced him and said firmly, "You must go and tell your family and everyone you know what God has done for you." Reluctantly, the man went on his way, and BB growled.

Back in the cave, they stood quietly for a moment.

"Children, the lamb of God is not just a sinless nobody. He is loved. Jesus is God's only and beloved Son. He is Mary's son and Joseph's adopted son. He has brothers and sisters, other children that Mary and Joseph had after he was born. And did you see how special he was to his disciples? Men, women, and children adore him. The Lamb of God, who takes away the sin of the world, is even more loved than that little lamb that was slain in the Garden of Eden. That makes his sacrifice all the more precious."

BB growled again, and the children were standing on either side of him at the foot of three tall crosses. They dug their hands into BB's fur as they looked at Jesus, nailed to the middle one. Was that really him? Their eyes filled with tears. They wanted to cry out like the women, who stood nearby. This man on the cross

didn't even look like Jesus! His face was badly beaten; his whole body was bruised. His blood trickled down from the top of his head, where they had placed a crown of thorns, to his nailed feet, dripping onto the ground below.

The twins remembered the first blood that was shed, the innocent lamb in the Garden of Eden. This was worse, but somehow, they knew this had to happen, or all was lost forever. Their hearts ached with sorrow and yet swelled with love for him.

The sky became violently dark, and the ground began to shake under their feet. They wept and clung to BB. Jesus said, "It is finished," and they saw his head drop. The women wailed. A man put his arms around them. The heavens thundered, rain poured down, and they became part of the streams of water, flowing into the ground, falling, falling, down they went. The twins were too heartbroken to be afraid. They just held on to BB.

They landed in a dark place that smelled terrible. Jesus stood in front of Satan, who sat on a huge throne and laughed hideously at him, commanding him to bow before him. Jesus looked beaten, pale, and was weighed down by a huge, dark sack. He stumbled toward the throne, dropped the sack, and began to dump its contents at the feet of Satan. It looked and smelled like horse manure.

Instead of being appalled, Satan reveled in it! He scooped it up and laughed, covering himself with it. "Ha! The glory of my kingdom!" With each handful, he cried out, "Oh, the love of money! Lying… stealing…murder of the innocents. Lust and immorality! Idolatry and rebellion. Witchcraft and sorcery! All my false religions and diabolical philosophies." He laughed a horrifying laugh. "Diseases and sickness and pain – the torture of these despicable humans," and he glared at Jesus, "especially you and your people!"

Jesus stepped back and whispered, "Yes. Sin belongs to you." At that moment, a brilliant light pierced the dark place and hit Jesus in his heart, then covered his whole body. He breathed deep and stood tall, hands raised, weeping and laughing with joy. "Abba! My Father!" He turned and looked at BB and the children, and his laughter was contagious. They began to laugh with him, and BB danced his bear jig.

Then Jesus whirled around to face Satan, who cowered in panic. "I'm taking what is legally mine," and Jesus took keys from Satan's gnarled fingers. Then Jesus flew to a large door that was hanging in the air, separated from where Satan was. With one of the keys, Jesus unlocked the door, and walls around what seemed to be a huge container fell away, revealing a multitude of people. They stared at Jesus. The twins gasped. There was John the Baptist! They wondered, *Could that man with the long, white beard be Moses? Is that beautiful woman Esther?*

"Beloved!" Jesus roared. "You know who I AM: Yeshua Hamashiach, the Lamb of God you believed would shed his blood and pay for your sins once and for all time, so you could be forgiven and restored to our Father. I give you the Good News: It is finished! Now enter into the fullness of joy in my kingdom forever!" Then he breathed on them and joyous cries of worship erupted. Everyone wanted to hug him.

Eventually, Jesus flew back to Satan, who had taken the form of a serpent again and was trying to slither away. Jesus walked over to the wriggling snake and crushed its head with his foot. Another swell of praise filled the place, and the twins jumped up and down, clapping their hands. They knew Satan was still around, but he no longer had any power or authority over Jesus and His followers.

Then Jesus, followed by the saints he had breathed upon, began to rise – up, up, up they went, and the twins held tightly to BB as they followed. In a moment, they were standing outside the tomb, where the disciples of Jesus had laid his dead body three days ago. They saw a troop of Roman soldiers, paralyzed on the ground, watch in shock as a mighty angel rolled the mammoth stone away from the opening of the tomb. Then Jesus emerged. He had scars in his hands and feet, and his prayer shawl nearly covered his face. BB growled.

"Oh, don't bring us back yet!" the twins cried.

8
The Decison

BB laughed and shook his head. "Let us sit one last time together," he said.

They sat on the cave floor as Josh blurted out, "We want to see more, BB! We want to see everything Jesus did after he was raised from the dead and where he is now!"

"Yes, BB! Let us see more of Jesus, please," implored Rachel.

"How would you like to be with Jesus forever?" asked BB. "Would that be better than a pirate's chest of gold, silver, and precious gems?"

Rachel cried, "Oh yes, BB!"

"Jesus is the treasure," said Josh.

"Jesus is the center of the treasure," answered BB.

"What do you mean?" asked Josh.

"Do you remember when we saw, in the Garden of Eden, that one decision made everything go wrong?"

"Yes."

"And then I told you that God would provide one decision to make everything right?"

"Uh huh."

"When you decide to give your life to Jesus, it is because he has become your greatest treasure, but there's more. All along, everything God the Father, Jesus the

Son, and the Holy Spirit have done to rescue you from sin and Satan was because you were their treasure. When you make Jesus the greatest treasure in your life, then you will understand what a great treasure you are to God. Josh, you will know what a great treasure Rachel is to God, and Rachel, you will know what a great treasure Josh is to God. You will know that the meaning of your life is to love God and his people in everything you say and do. From that comes every blessing, joy, and honor."

"BB, I don't want to go another minute without Jesus as my treasure," said Rachel, tears in her eyes.

"Me too," said Josh.

"Well then, you are making the most important decision a human can make. Just pray what I pray: Dear Heavenly Father... I'm sorry for my sins, and I don't want to ever be separated from you...Thank you for sending your Son Jesus to die for my sins… I believe you raised him from the dead to give me a new life, to make my spirit alive to you…and from now on, Jesus is the Lord of my life…Thank you for saving me, Father! I pray this in the name of Jesus. Amen.”

Josh and Rachel looked at each other in wonder. Did they look different? A new peace filled their hearts, and they began to giggle. They fell into a long group hug with BB, crying, “Thank you! Thank you, BB!”

As they let go of him, BB began to fade. They tried to grab hold of him again, but their arms and hands went right through him. What was happening? Before they could cry out, he looked in their eyes and said, “Don’t be sad or afraid. I am called Bible Bear because I help children understand God’s words. But your spirits are alive now, so you will hear his words in your hearts. Read them, live your lives by them, and treasure them always. God's words will give meaning to every part of your lives."

Then BB completely vanished, and two books sat where he had been. One was green and one was red. Each was titled, *Holy Bible*. Josh and Rachel picked them up and held them to their hearts. They wept with joy, foreheads touching.

Eventually, each opened their Bible and read silently. Josh read, "I am the way and the truth and the life. No one comes to the Father but by me." The words resounded in his spirit and filled his heart. Rachel read, "Take my yoke upon you and learn of me, for I am gentle and humble in heart, and you will find rest for your soul."

"Josh, it's true. I hear Jesus speaking to me inside my spirit, in my heart."

"Me too. It's like a…a miracle."

Clutching their new treasure, each stood and looked around the room one last time. It was bare. Even the basket of nuts and fruit was gone. The pool of water was dried up. The light in the ceiling was gone, but sunlight shone from across the room. They put their Bibles, their flashlights, and their water bottles in their backpacks and walked toward the light. It was a doorway to the world they had left only a few hours ago. How different it seemed now!

They passed through the doorway, and it closed up behind them. They looked at each other, giggled, and put on their backpacks.

"Do you think this happened to Mom and Dad?" asked Josh.

"And Grandma and Grandpa!" said Rachel.

"I can't wait to ask them," smiled Josh.

"Me too," Rachel nodded.

Walking home in the warmth of the sun, they talked about all they had seen and heard with BB. They would never forget him and how he had brought them to Jesus in such a special way. They didn't need the map to retrace their steps, as they remembered the way perfectly. The three trees, the large boulder, the ancient Indian trail, the tree with the arrowhead etched on it, and the holly bush, where they turned west to the log that crossed the stream. Then they followed the stream south until they saw Grandma and Grandpa's driveway across the road.

As they hiked the slight incline of Grandma and Grandpa's long driveway, it dawned on them: It was just late afternoon! They marveled at how they had traveled to so many places, that it seemed they had been away for days, and God had done it all in one afternoon. They looked at each other and laughed when they heard in their spirits, "I sit outside of time and am the same yesterday, today, and forever."

There were many questions for Grandma and Grandpa, Mom and Dad, in the days ahead. Many good times and tough times, joys and sorrows, were in their futures. But they had the treasure in their hearts, Jesus, who imparted meaning to each day and into eternity.

About the Authors

R. J. Albanese graduated from the University of Virginia and became the vice president of marketing for a new and highly successful computer software company specializing in artificial intelligence. Later, he left that company to attend Rhema Bible Training Center in Tulsa, Oklahoma, and after that he did mission work in Central America and worked in crusades around the world. He returned to the United States to work with his father's law firm, doing title work until he retired. Always active in his church, he taught children for twenty years, and he still teaches whenever he's given the opportunity. He participates in prayer teams and also performs various acts of service in his church. He has written two other books: *Who You Are and What You Should Be Doing* and *The Meaning of Life*. Ron is married and has a daughter and a step-daughter. You can contact him through his website:

www.rjalbanese.com

E. T. Sherman graduated from Northwestern University and worked as a legal assistant until she married and had two children, a son and a daughter. After being divorced, she returned to work but soon left the legal field for Christian publishing, working first as a developmental editor and then acquisitions editor. Employed by publishers and later working as a freelancer, she has edited or ghostwritten over 250 books, which include authors from various denominations and theological persuasions. She ministered with Native American Christians and was an instructor at Two Rivers Native American Training Center. In churches she has attended, she has preached on Sunday morning and taught the Bible to adults, youth, and children for over twenty years. She is active in prayer team ministry, as well as helping those in need. Both her children are married, and she has five incredible grandchildren. She can be contacted through www.rjalbanese.com.